TEN
TERRIBLE
DINOSAURS

For my little monsters

TEN
TERRIBLE
DINOSAURS

Paul Stickland

PUFFIN BOOKS

10 terrible dinosaurs

until there were...

9 enormous dinosaurs

—their dancing was just great,

but one was much too spiky,

so then there were...

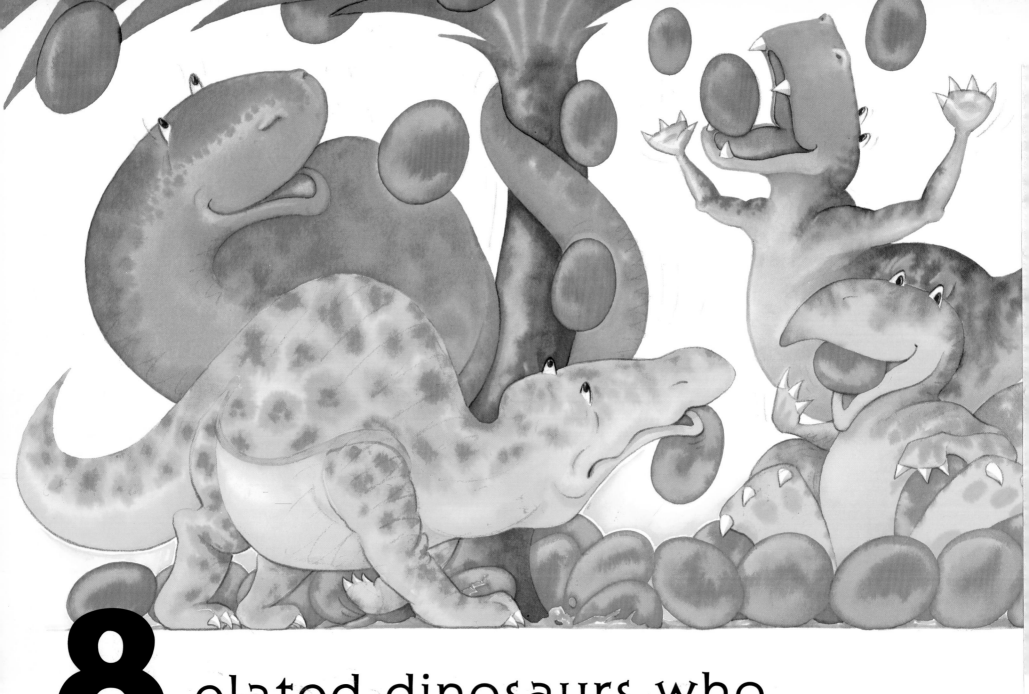

8 elated dinosaurs who

thought they were in heaven,

but one nearly popped,

so then there were...

7 silly dinosaurs,

playing goofy tricks,

but one went too far,

so then there were...

6 stomping dinosaurs

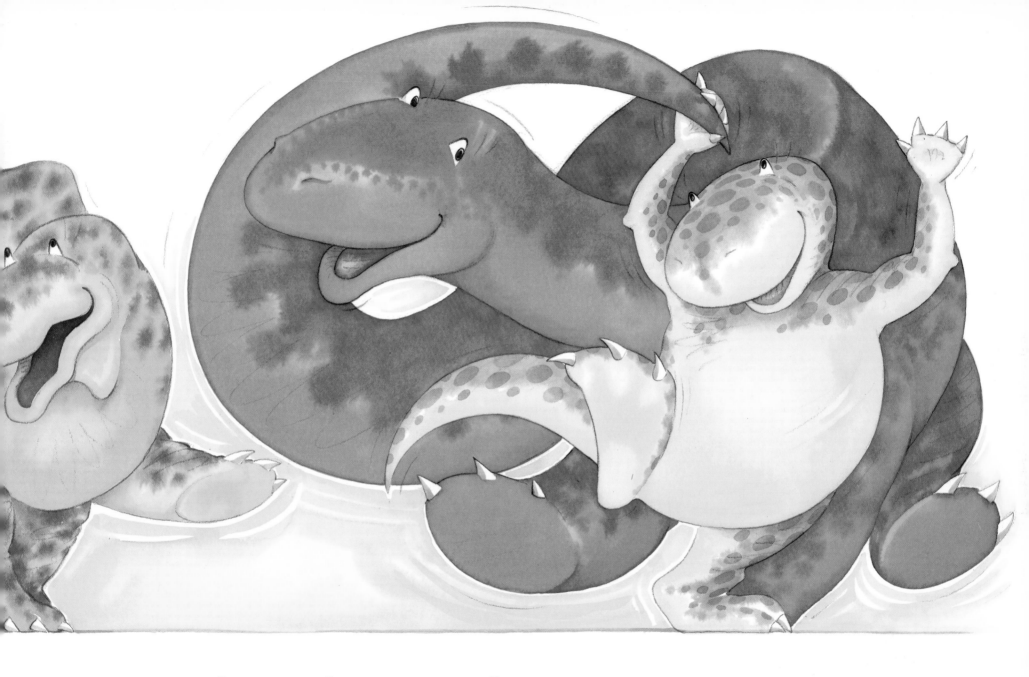

who danced a crazy jive,

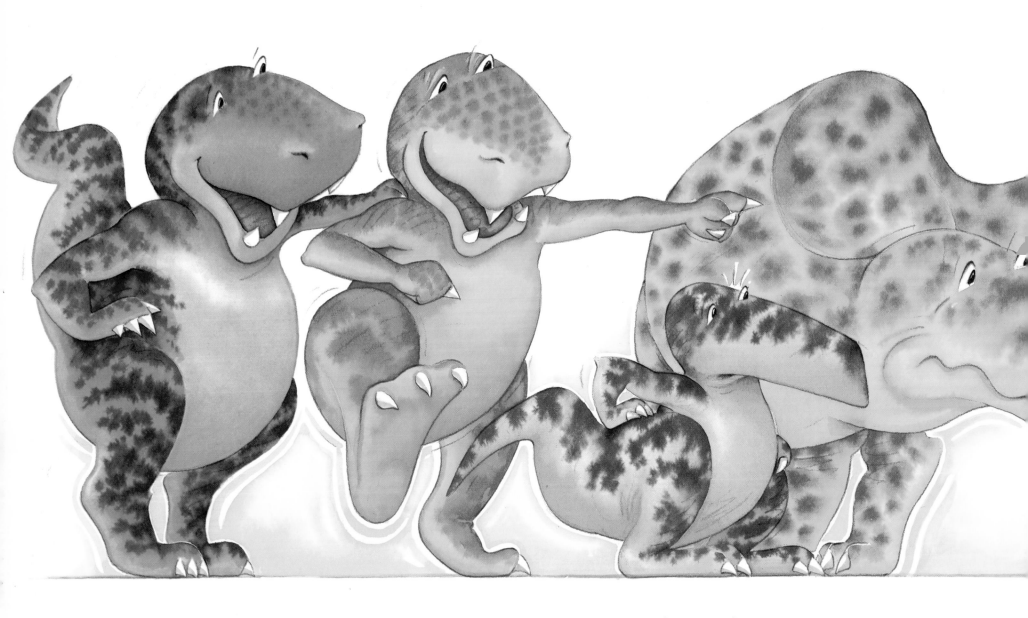

but one got tangled up,

so then there were...

5 feisty dinosaurs

stamping on the floor.

"Quiet down!" cried someone's mom,

and then there were...

4 fearless dinosaurs

swinging from a tree

but one got stuck

—so then there were...

3 thundering dinosaurs

who flapped and almost flew.

One took off!

So then there were...

2 testy dinosaurs,

tired of all the fun;

one got taken home,

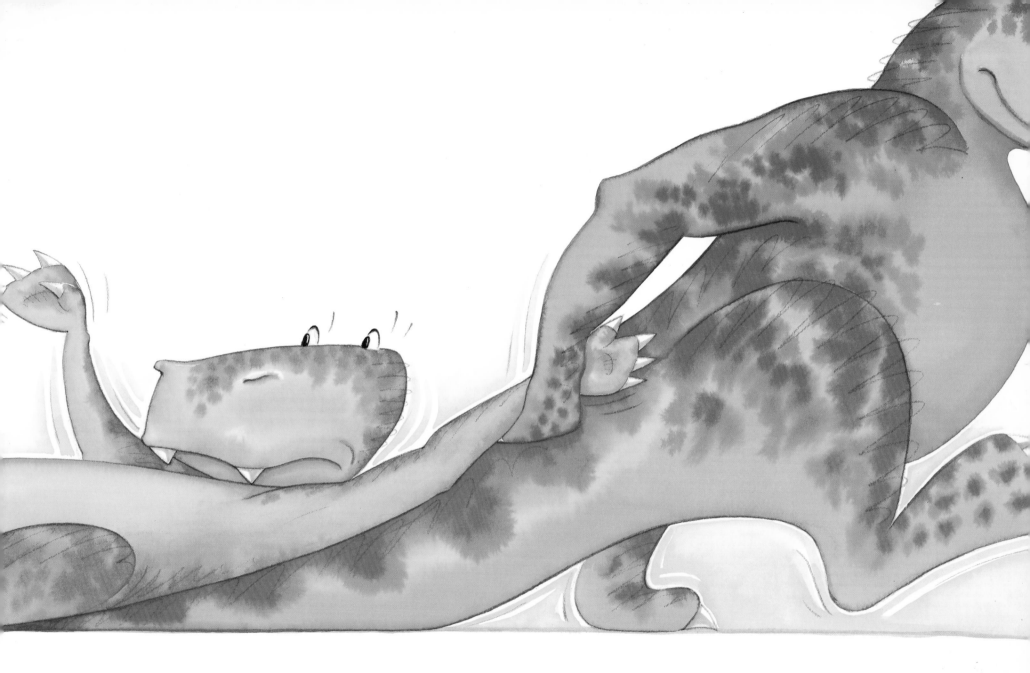

so then there was...

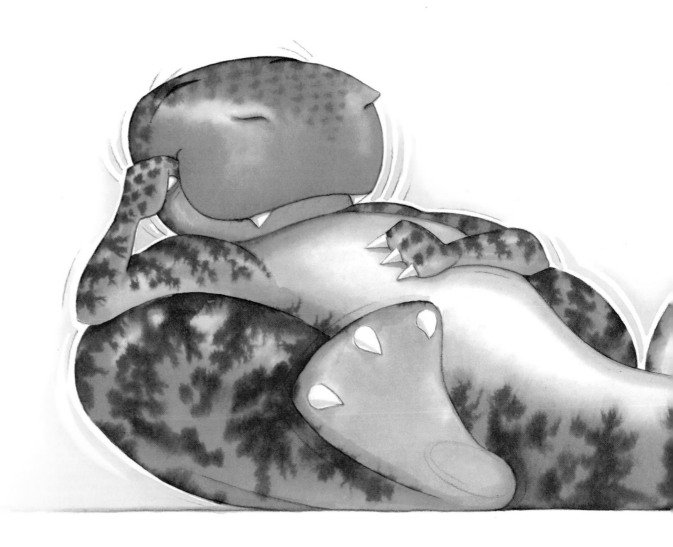

1 weary dinosaur

who soon began to snore.

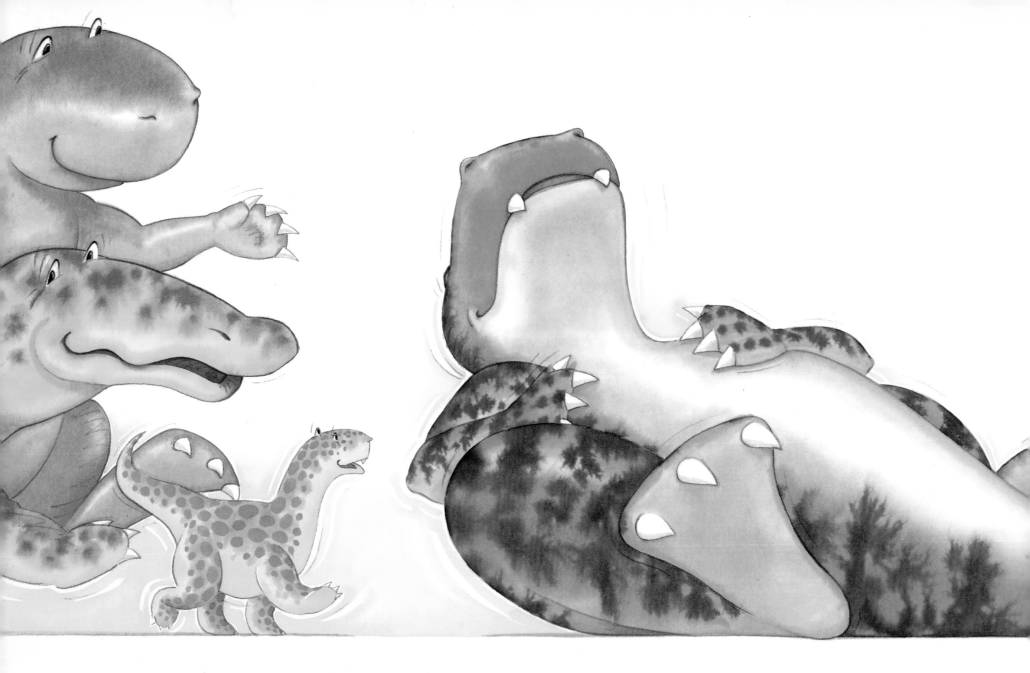

His friends sneaked up behind him

and suddenly yelled . . .

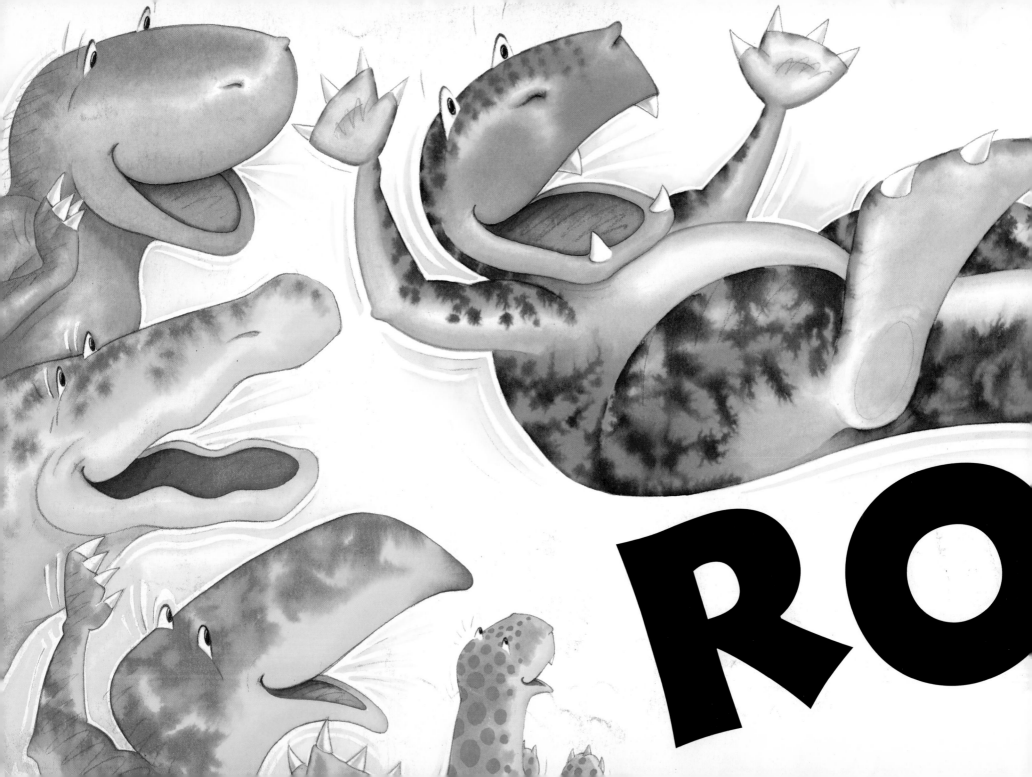

PUFFIN BOOKS
Published by the Penguin Group
Penguin Putnam Books for Young Readers, 345 Hudson Street, New York, New York 10014, U.S.A.
Penguin Books Ltd, 27 Wrights Lane, London W8 5TZ, England
Penguin Books Australia Ltd, Ringwood, Victoria, Australia
Penguin Books Canada Ltd, 10 Alcorn Avenue, Toronto, Ontario, Canada M4V 3B2
Penguin Books (N.Z.) Ltd, 182-190 Wairau Road, Auckland 10, New Zealand

Penguin Books Ltd, Registered Offices: Harmondsworth, Middlesex, England

First published by Ragged Bears Limited, Hampshire, England, 1997
First published in the United States of America by Dutton Children's Books,
a member of Penguin Putnam Inc., 1997
Published by Puffin Books, a division of Penguin Putnam Books for Young Readers, 2000

5 7 9 10 8 6 4

THE LIBRARY OF CONGRESS HAS CATALOGED THE DUTTON EDITION AS FOLLOWS:
Stickland, Paul.
Ten terrible dinosaurs / Paul Stickland—1st American ed.   p.   cm.
Summary: A group of rollicking dinosaurs counts down from
ten to one as it introduces subtraction to the reader.
[1. Subtraction—Fiction. 2. Dinosaurs—Fiction. 3. Counting. 4. Stories in rhyme.] I. Title.
PZ8.3.S856Tg 1997 [E]—dc21 97-214697 CIP AC
ISBN 0-525-45905-7

Puffin Books ISBN 0-14-056770-4

Printed in China